GREG PIZZOLI

LUCKY DUCK

Alfred A. Knopf New York

Susan the duck was feeling a bit unlucky.

The roller skates she ordered online
were two sizes too big.

"I have the worst luck!" said Susan
as she pulled on another pair of socks.

Just then, the doorbell rang.

"Congratulations!

It's your lucky day!" said the wolf at the door.
"You've won!"

"I did? I won?" asked Susan.
"What did I win?"

"You have won this fabulous pot!" said the wolf.
"Perfect for making soup! Congratulations again!
You are one lucky duck!"

Susan did feel lucky.
It was a very nice pot.
A little big for her kitchen,
but still very nice.

"Thank you!" she said to the wolf.
The rest of the morning she felt very lucky.

But just before lunch, her luck turned.
Her kitchen lightbulb burned out.

"Of all the bad luck!"
said Susan as she got out
a new bulb and her ladder.

Then the doorbell rang.

"Congratulations!
It's your lucky day!" said the wolf.
"You've won!"

"But . . . ," said Susan,
"I already won.
I already have a pot."

"Of course!" said the wolf. "And now you have won
these wonderful onions! Great for soup!
What a lucky duck you are!"

"Oh!" said Susan.
She liked onions.
And she loved soup.
This was a lot of onions
to eat all by herself,
but still, she felt lucky.

"Thank you again, Mr. Wolf!"
Susan called as she carried
the onions to her cupboard.

A little while later, she was making a sandwich when she saw that her pickle jar was empty.

"No pickles?!" cried Susan. "What bad luck!"

But she felt better
after the wolf showed up
with a big bunch of celery.

By the afternoon, Susan was feeling unlucky.
She had lost her favorite marble.

But then the wolf brought her carrots,
and she felt lucky again.
Maybe I will make that soup, thought Susan.

That evening, Susan invited some
friends to share her soup.

While she was talking on the phone,
she discovered a nest of hornets in the tree
behind her house. "Just my rotten luck!" she said.

She was in the kitchen looking for her bug spray when she heard a knock at the door.

"It's open! Come in!" yelled Susan.

"Hello, duck," said the wolf.
"Are you making the soup?"

"Yes," said Susan, "thanks to you!
I have added the onions, the celery,
and the carrots to the big pot.

"I invited some friends for dinner,
and you should join us. I think it
will be a very nice soup."

"Yes, I'm sure it will," said the wolf.

Susan gulped. "Duck soup?"

"That's right," said the wolf.
"Today is MY lucky day!"

The wolf snarled.
He grinned at Susan
with his jagged teeth.

"Duck soup is
my favorite dish."

"Oh no!" yelped Susan.
"My luck has run out!"

And then . . .

The wolf slipped
on Susan's marble,

and he fell

SLIP!

headfirst into the
empty pickle jar!

FLOP!

Then he banged
into the ladder,

BANG!

lost his balance,
and jammed his foot

into one of Susan's
two-sizes-too-big
roller skates.

POP!

Susan gasped as the wolf flew out
the back door, slammed into the tree,
and smacked right into the hornets' nest.

And then that rotten wolf
rolled down the hill,
never to be seen again.

Just then, the doorbell rang.

Susan's friends had arrived for dinner.

"Welcome!" said Susan.
"The soup is almost ready."

Susan looked
around the table
and smiled.

She felt
very,
very
lucky.

The End

For Fiona

THIS IS A BORZOI BOOK PUBLISHED BY ALFRED A. KNOPF
Copyright © 2024 by Greg Pizzoli
All rights reserved. Published in the United States by Alfred A. Knopf, an imprint of
Random House Children's Books, a division of Penguin Random House LLC, New York.
Knopf, Borzoi Books, and the colophon are registered trademarks of Penguin Random House LLC.
Visit us on the Web! rhcbooks.com
Educators and librarians, for a variety of teaching tools, visit us at RHTeachersLibrarians.com

Library of Congress Cataloging-in-Publication Data is available upon request.
ISBN 978-0-593-64977-0 (trade) — ISBN 978-0-593-64978-7 (lib. bdg.) — ISBN 978-0-593-64979-4 (ebook)

The text of this book is hand-lettered based on 19-point Futura.
The illustrations were drawn with pencil, brush, and Photoshop.
The book was printed in four spot colors.
Edited by Rotem Moscovich
Book design by Martha M. Rago

MANUFACTURED IN CHINA
10 9 8 7 6 5 4 3 2 1
First Edition